Discovering childhood

Discovering childhood

ALDIVAN Torres

Canary Of Joy

Contents

1   "Discovering childhood"   1

{ 1 }

"Discovering childhood"

Aldivan Torres

Discovering childhood

Author: Aldivan Torres
@2019- Aldivan Torres
All rights reserved

This book, including all its parts, is copyrighted and cannot be reproduced without the author's permission, resold or transferred.

Aldivan Torres, a native of Brazil, is a consolidated writer in several genres. To date it has titles published in dozens of languages. From an early age, he was always a lover of the art of writing having consolidated a professional career from the second half of 2013. He hopes with his writings to contribute to international culture, arousing the pleasure of reading those who do not yet have the habit. Your mission is to win the hearts of each of your readers. In addition to literature, its main tastes are music, travel, friends, family, and the pleasure of living. "For literature, equality, fraternity, justice, dignity, and honor of the human being always" is his motto.

"No one lights a lamp to cover it with a canister or put it under the bed. He puts it on the lamp, so that everyone who comes in will see the light. In fact, all that is hidden must become manifest; and everything that is in secret, must become known and clearly manifest. Therefore, pay attention as you hear: for those who have something will be given even more; for the one who does not have, will be taken away even what he thinks he has." (LC 8.16-18)

"Discovering childhood"
Discovering childhood
Dedication and thanks
Thanks
1-Childhood
1.1-Fundão, August 1, 1900-
1.2-Celebration
1.3-Feast of Baptism
1.4- The first toys
1.5-The disease and the first word
1.6-Finally, standing
1.7-Visit of relatives
1.8-The two-year period
1.9-The first day at school
1.10-The first beating
1.11-The birth of the second child
1.12-Three more years are over
1.13-Some interesting experiences in the lives of the two brothers
1.14-The discovery of love
1.15- The new routine

Discovering childhood

1.16-The stories of Filomena
1.17-The code of conduct of Filomena
1.18-Hunter Stories
1.19-Farewell
1.20-End of childhood

1-Childhood

1.1-FUNDÃO, AUGUST 1, 1900-

It was a sunny Wednesday afternoon. The couple Filomena and Jilmar were resting in front of their small and simple house. They had already completed a year of marriage and change of the headquarters of the municipality Cimbres (Current Fishing), and were pleased despite the great financial difficulties that were. Jilmar, still in his time of dating, had worked as a convict as a cargo assistant to raise money and buy a small piece of land and had been helped by the then bride Filomena who made lace. When they raised enough money, they got married, moved to the place, and started a life together. With little time, Filomena had found himself pregnant.

This same afternoon, he had completed the long nine months of waiting. Resting and thinking about the future, suddenly, Filomena began to feel the pain, asked for help to her husband who went on fire, on horseback, looking for a midwife. The young Victor hurried to debut in a world full of miseries, difficulties, but which was also beautiful and pleasurable. At the time she was alone, Filomena began to recite prayers addressed to Our lady of good childbirth, and they somewhat alleviated her anxiety and pain. When she least expected, her husband Jilmar returned with the grace midwife, took her to her room and thanks to the two after two harrowing hours, the boy was finally born.

There began another spectacular trajectory of the Torres lineage, a special race of human beings, full of various gifts. Over time, his inclination to the hidden arts would be revealed and only God would know where it could go. For now, he would be raised by a love-filled couple who would teach him the basic concepts of survival, values, ethics and how to behave in a society still unequal in the early twentieth century.

1.2 - CELEBRATION

After the birth, Jilmar and Filomena began to worry about the newborn's food and clothing. That's when they had an idea: to call some acquaintances from the region who had a greater possession to participate in a small celebration and for them to reciprocate with gifts. That's what they did. A week later, they opened the doors of their small, simple home and welcomed their friends. Among them, the unmarried cousins of Filomena, Angelica and Bartlomy and other relatives of Jilmar.

Everyone who showed up was well-received. Out of curiosity, they looked at the baby, praised its attributes and reciprocated with various gifts of utility. The couple thanked and paid attention to everyone. In the end, they served a small banquet, which, although simple, was much appreciated. When the food ran out, the conversation continued to swirl for a long time on general issues including politics, news. So, time has passed. Near dusk, those present were saying goodbye, and finally, only Jilmar, Filomena and Angelica were left. The latter, before leaving, approached the baby, touched him and in a cry made a prophecy: ——This yes will be proud of the Torres race, it will be a pathfinder of his time!

The parents didn't quite understand the outburst, but they thanked them anyway. When Angelica left, the two were alone, took the opportunity to eat, date and then sleep because at that time, in a distant place, there were not many leisure options.

1.3 - FEAST OF BAPTISM

From a traditionally Catholic family, like the vast majority of people in the interior of Brazil, the first initiation of the newborn

Discovering childhood

Vítor into religion was organized, that is, his baptism. For the occasion were invited relatives and friends, including the bridesmaids and a godfather.

It was August 15, 1900, another Wednesday. All the guests of the occasion and the boy's parents went to the fishing house, more exactly the cathedral. At the agreed time, everyone was present, scattered on the benches of the Church. But the priest hadn't arrived yet. They waited another thirty minutes, vicar Freitas arrived, and began the celebration. During ink minutes, preached his ideology and explained the responsibilities of all present. When everything was made explicit, the ritual continued and, in the end, consecrated Vítor. During surrender to Christ, a roar was heard in heaven and everyone was surprisingly. What would become of that intriguing boy's life?

Doubt would remain in everyone's mind until it grows. Meanwhile, he would learn from the closest and with life every detail of the world. After an adult, he would decide his destiny, through his respective choices. Because that's what the human being is, it's free to love, hate, build or destroy. We are the main responsible for our destiny. Keep up, reader.

1.4- THE FIRST TOYS

Two months have passed since Victor's birth and the children's day is finally approaching. Despite the delicate financial situation, Jilmar arranged with his wife a walk in the city's playground on this critical date. On the day and time combined, the two moved, riding a horse and taking the baby. Overcoming natural barriers such as dust, the loss-making road and the scorching sun they arrive at the head of the house after an hour of much struggle.

From the entrance of the city to the park is another twenty minutes' drive. On the way, they meet acquaintances and relatives, greet them and wish them a happy children's day. They reciprocate and wish for luck and success. Continue the journey, find a pub and decide to stop to rest. Made the decision, disassemble, attach the rope of the animal in a bush so that it pastes a little, and they go to the establishment. With a few more steps, they arrive, sit at the table, are attended and ask for a juice and a quick snack. While they wait for food, they date, and they talk to each other.

"What's up, woman, Victor, and you're all right? They look a little too rosy. (Jilmar)

"We're a little exhausted and warm. It's not easy to travel with the sun beating head-on, but we survived. It's all worth it when we're about to live happy and intense family moments. (Filomena)

"This season does not forgive, but I agree that it is worth it. Even though we're against it, we're happy, and we're a real family. I can't wait to see this kid running through the mud of our house, hugging us and calling us parents. (Jilmar)

"Easy, old man. This still takes a little time. For now, we must prepare to offer the minimum conditions for it to develop. It's our mission from now on. (Filomena)

"Yes, of course. Soon I will prepare the land of the mowing next year. I hope it rains. Meanwhile, I'll keep working rented, for some of our land neighbors. One way or another we'll pass and with dignity. (Jilmar)

"I'm glad you're willing. I didn't regret marrying you because you've always shown yourself to be a warrior in this life without opportunities. Thank you for choosing me as a woman, too. (Filomena)

"I love you too. (Jilmar)

At this point, the two hug and kiss sweetly. Those present applaud the gesture, and it makes them blush. They are silent for a while, the snack, and juice arrive, begin to feed quietly planning the rest of the day. When they finish feeding, they call the attendant, pay the bill, get off the scene, get back on the horse and continue the journey. Now they'd only stop when they got to the right destination.

Returning to the path, hurry the trot. A few minutes after intense bumps through the streets of the small town of Pesqueira, passing through the cherry neighborhood, downtown, and meadow finally they arrive. At the entrance to the park, they take off the horse, trap it to a nearby tree, pay for the entrance tickets, and enter. They start to go through all the places, making the most of the toys. When they arrive in front of a stall, they are interested, appreciate the local handicrafts and, in a gesture of affection, With the rest of the little money he had, Jilmar buys a gift for his wife, a dress of the time and for his son, buys a rattle (Maraca) to distract himself. In gratitude, Filomena hugs him and kisses him. They continue to enjoy the toys, walk through various places within the park, time passes and already late, decide to return to the house. Quickly, if they drive to the exit, ride the horse again and start making their way back. They would take about the same time from the way, in return, but it had even been worth it. They lived special moments, on such an important day, the children's day and with their first baby.

1.5-THE DISEASE AND THE FIRST WORD

After the walk in the park, the family formed by Filomena, Jilmar and Vítor returned to their normal routine. Jilmar continued preparing the land to plant waiting for the winter weather and consequently enough sun and rain; Filomena, with her work as a housewife, lace maker and mother; And Victor, even unconscious, discovering a new world, diverse, complicated, but at the same time beautiful. So, time went by.

Exactly six months after his birth, Vítor had a small virus, fell into fever and his parents, worried, immediately took him to the municipal hospital of the headquarters of his municipality of Cimbres. The trip on horseback took thirty minutes and when they arrived at the destination, entered a room and waited another hour. Thereafter, the boy was finally medicated being referred to a room, staying under observation. One of the parents was allowed to stay with him. They chose Filomena because she was her mother and more intimate with him. At one point, the nurses came in and suggested that Filomena go out for a while, rest and feed. She accepted the suggestion but by the time she was going to retire, Victor stirred a lot, cried, squeaked, and in an effort on human for his age, he cried out his first word:

"Mother!

The scene thrilled everyone, especially Filomena for having the grace to hear her name pronounced by her baby who thought she was sick. In an impetus, he kissed him, hugged him and promised to always be by his side, in the good times and bad. With these words, the boy calmed down, relaxed and finally fell asleep. So, Filomena took advantage and left a little, fed, talked to her husband and returned to the observation room before he woke up. You spent the rest of the night with him. The other day, when it dawned, he was discharged from the hospital and only then was it possible to return to the house. With that, they would continue in their simple life always but happy.

1.6 - FINALLY, STANDING

Time passed a while. Winter came, it rained a lot and the Torres family, in the person of Jilmar, placed their mowing, planting the main basic food products such as beans, corn, sweet potatoes, cassava, manioc, watermelon, pumpkins, melon, among others. With three months to go, corn and beans could already be harvested. With profit, they would have their basic needs met for at least a year. Relates the boy, he grew up in sight, began to crawl and daily his father was busy taking him from one side to another trying to teach him to walk. He had already made two attempts, but the two resulted in failure, the boy had taken two tumbles and thereafter, he was more careful and would only try once more when the boy was ready.

Exactly a year after his birth, Victor was already holding on to the walls, and when he became a little firmer his father stood in front of him and called him. Even incredulous, the boy risked: He took a step, two, and when he least expected, walked firmly, approached and hugged his father, called his name. It was the first achievement of many of that poor but blessed boy of God and full of gifts. The future was now in your hands. Would it be realized even in a time so full of misery, injustice, and so delayed culturally? Keep up, reader.

1.7-VISIT OF RELATIVES

The event that caused Victor's first steps on his feet and alone occurred in the morning. After celebrating the fact, Jilmar went to take care of his duties in the swidden and Filomena began to fulfill his obligations also that was to clean the house, prepare lunch and still keep an eye on Vítor. With the effort of the two and luckily helping, everything was fine.

Some time passes, it was approaching noon, Jilmar returns home and finds everything in order. As he was hungry, he goes straight to the small kitchen, greets his wife and son, sits at the table, is kindly served by his wife and begins to taste her always attractive seasoning, consisting of beans, flour, sun meat complemented by typical wild fruits. All basic, but very tasteful.

At one point, Jilmar, pulls conversation with his beloved.

"And then woman, tell me the news. What else did our pupil learn today?

"The usual. Like any boy your age, you touched everything in your power, and I to avoid a bigger disaster gave you a few spankings. Luckily, it was enough for him to calm down. (Filomena)

"Have more patience woman. He's still a baby. Of course, if necessary, we'll apply a concealer to you. But it's still early. (Jilmar)

"Talking is easy. You're not the one who has to stand back and running after him avoiding something worse. Patience has a limit and I still have to take care of my obligations. (Filomena)

"I get that. I live in your hands the task of uplifting him. Just don't overdo it. I've been really busy lately, working for everyone. Bones of the craft. (Jilmar)

"I know, and I don't criticize you for it. Someone has to put food in the house. On the contrary, I appreciate your dedication to this family, and for making me so happy. (Filomena)

Tears flow down Filomena's face and emotion dominates the moment. Jilmar pauses the food, approached it, hugs it and kisses it. In an impulse, Victor also approaches and the hug becomes triple. There was a family of battlers who were willing to face any kind of challenge and perform despite all the difficulties imposed by the time. When the hug ends, they part a little and Jilmar continues to make his meal. At the end of lunch, Vítor feels sleepy, Filomena puts him to sleep and the couple enjoy resting and date a little. Shortly after, the afternoon begins.

Around three o'clock in the afternoon, someone knocks on the door, they get out of bed, and they're going to answer. When opening the door, they have a pleasant surprise: They were the closest cousins of Filomena, Angelica and Bartlomy who unceremoniously invited themselves in. After the initial greetings, they sit on the available stools and start a good conversation, explain the reason for the visit (Victor's one-year anniversary), and finally deliver the gifts. The couple thanks, Vítor wakes up with the movement, appears in the room, and receives the affection of the gifts. As a good hostess, Filomena will prepare a snack for visitors to thank so much kindness. Fifteen minutes later, come back with everything ready. The visits are served and the conversation continues on all the news of the region. After the snack, they return to the room and the conversation continues, each speaking a little of their life. At one point, Jilmar says goodbye to take care of some to-do. Angelica and Bartlomy continue with Filomena. When the sunset, they say goodbye, gives the young Victor a hug and finally leave. They promise to come back another day. Jilmar returns home, waits for dinner is ready, feeds, the lamp is lit, and two hours later they all go to sleep lacking entertainment and leisure option. Their routine of fighting and overcoming would continue on the other days.

1.8-THE TWO-YEAR PERIOD

With each passing day, Victor grew in stature and wisdom closely accompanied by his parents. This period was critical and fundamental in the setting of values for any individual and for this reason, Filomena and Jilmar, struggled to give a good basis of education for the same. With each slip of his, the same was corrected and even without having an exact awareness of what was happening the same absorbed the knowledge. It was two years, and it was enrolled in the school.

The current moment of the Torres family was one of stability. They continued to live on agriculture in their small place and the profits of the mowing were sufficient to sustain them from the basics. In addition to the mowing, Jilmar earned some change working rented to neighbors of land and Filomena, made lace crafts and raised some animals such as chickens, ducks, turkeys, and sheep that helped in the sustenance. They weren't rich, but they weren't hungry like they used to. They were still happy, which was the most important thing.

One day, good news: Filomena thought she was pregnant with her second child. Although this meant greater expense, the fact was celebrated like never. It would be wonderful a company for Vítor, distract him in the games, in the adventures and help him to grow even more. It would further strengthen the identity of such a struggling and suffering family. The Torres family.

1.9 - THE FIRST DAY AT SCHOOL

February begins and with it the school period. On the day scheduled for the beginning, Filomena tried to fix her son Vítor in the best possible way and when it was ready, the two left together for the house of Genoveva, where the school group operated improvised. The residence was located on the side of the main dirt road, which was going towards the headquarters of the municipality. From Filomena's house to hers were about forty minutes standing, and they had to make this journey every day. However, it would be worth the knowledge and culture assimilated.

With the previous thought, the two walks along the bumpy road and at one point reach the main road. Without obstacles, the two speed up their steps, meet other children and adults who also leave for school and decide to walk together. To be distracted, adults talk a little and pass on instructions to their children that they seem to understand despite their young age.

The walk continues. Soon after, young children feel tired and parents are forced to carry them. But not for long. Ten minutes later, they are approaching the rural school of the Fundão site and with a few more steps arrive in front of her. It makes the call of the enrolled, all respond, and are sent to a small room with some wallets. In total, sixteen (the number of students in the primary study that year). Parents stay out of it.

As there were four grades with four students each, she had to prepare a different class for each group of these and started with Victor's class that represented the first grade, not yet literate. He took four feathers and four cartridges and as he taught them how to handle these writing instruments, he showed the letters of the alphabet. As it was only the first day, no demands were made to the students unless they paid attention to what was quite difficult because they were small children who were never distant from their parents. But all this was considered despite the teacher's rigidity. The expected forty minutes of class passed quickly without major complications. In sequence, the lesson of another series began, but those of the first had to attend as well. And so on.

Everything went very well in class until a fourth grader missed a basic question and Genoveva, using the authority that the teachers had at the time, sampled him using the spanking. This was enough to scare the little ones, including Victor, who began calling for their parents insistently. To control the situation, Genoveva Garcia finished the exhibition class and took all the students to nature, a forest near his home, taught about the fauna and flora, took them to the swidden that was very close to his house and put the boys in the grip of animals. That's how I solved the problems. When the time came, they returned to the room, fired them, the little children were handed over to their parents who were still waiting outside, and they all returned to the house. That's how a school at the site of that time worked and Victor would have to attend it every day.

1.10 - THE FIRST BEATING

Time went a little ahead. In the Torres family, everything went through the usual normal routine: Jilmar's work in agriculture and Filomena at home, Vítor's going to school, the pranks, the antics, and his growth in the eye. Everything led me to believe that everything would be fine all the time, but you never know what could happen.

A difficult phase begins in the life of little Victor, his special gifts begin to surface, which worries his parents a lot. They take him to a wise man. At the time, they are told not to worry because this was absolutely normal and that with a while, he would learn to control this power and use it to his advantage. It was a gift of fate and not a curse as they thought.

Each new day, Victor learned a little more about the other world: He had invisible friends, spoke to angels and messengers, received messages about his future and from his later descendant. Everything was too new for him and, following the advice of his parents, he didn't tell his secrets to anyone. Although this is absolutely normal in the spiritual lineage of his family, a lineage of seers.

The problem was his inexperience, and often he could not distinguish good company from bad ones. One day, guided by an inner voice, it was suggested that it throw away the food because it would be contaminated by bad fluids. Innocent, he let himself be carried away and performed the act in an oversight of his mother. Asked by his mother, he said it was for everyone's sake.

Instigated by anger and heartbreak because this was the only food available of the day, Filomena took the strap and gave her a few lashes, few but firm. He cried, squealed, blasphemed, but recognized that he deserved it despite his young age. The act was enough for him to have to take a bath with salt diluted in the water to relieve his pains. Helped by his mother, a little sorry, he was taken to bed to rest. This had been a painful lesson, and he certainly wouldn't make the same mistake twice.

1.11 - THE BIRTH OF THE SECOND CHILD

Nine months have passed. As last time, the pains of Filomena's birth began suddenly, and luckily, it was lunchtime and her husband was at home. Distressingly, he left the house, rode his horse and went to look for the midwife. Thirty minutes later, he returns with the same midwife who helped give birth to Victor who was called Grace, just in time. Filomena was taken to her room and the midwife assisted by Jilmar, brought to life the second son of the couple still unnamed. They put the baby in the basket, left the mother resting, left the room, Jilmar paid the midwife, thanked her, she said goodbye and finally left.

An hour later, Jilmar calls Victor who all the time was playing outside, and together they enter the room where the baby and the family matriarch were found. As they enter, they witness a wonderful scene: Filomena, with the baby on her lap, kissing him and blessing him. They approach, get emotional too, and together they make a quadruple hug. This moment lasts long enough for them to feel the great love that unites them. The Torres family was exceptional.

When the hug ends, they sit on the bed next to her and start a conversation.

"So, woman, do you know what your name is going to be? (Jilmar)

"I just decided. It will be called Raphael, like the angel who always protects us. (Filomena)

"Rafael. Who the one is that? (Spells Victor)

"It's your brother. (Filomena)

"And what is a brother? (Victor)

"Brother is the son of the same father and mother. (Explains with patience Jilmar)

"Oh, yes. (Victor)

Discovering childhood

The smart Vítor gives Rafael a kiss and leaves the room to play outside again with his imaginary horse. Meanwhile, Jilmar and Filomena continue to exchange ideas.

"I'm afraid that with Raphael's arrival, Victor will feel jealous and try to do something stupid. You know how temperamental he is. (Filomena)

"Don't worry about it. He's just a good-natured kid. We knew how to raise him. Just pay a little attention. (Jilmar guaranteed)

"You're right. Our son is special, has a gift, and we must always be by his side to guide. I hope he follows in his footsteps. (Filomena)

"It is only to follow the same formula of creation that has no error: Teach the precepts, the values of good, correcting failures, giving examples, encouraging you to always help others. Speaking of kids, when are we going to have the next one? (Jilmar)

"No way. Even though I love kids, I only want to have two. It's a lot of work and don't even try to convince me otherwise. (Filomena said)

"That's all right. We will avoid having new children as much as possible. I don't agree, but I accept your decision. (Jilmar)

"Thank you for understanding, love. (Filomena)

Filomena puts the newborn Rafael in the basket gives a kiss and a hug to her husband. From now on, their mission was twofold: Two beings depended on them to grow, form men, and win in life, despite all the difficulties of the time. In addition, they would always have to feed the relationship of love and affection so that they would reap complete happiness.

After the kiss and hug, they stimulate themselves, close the bedroom door, and enjoy free time to date and have sex, something they had not performed for a long time. After the consummate act, they nap and rest a little longer. After, Jilmar gets up and goes to take care of the house, the dinner and the smart boy he had. I would stay a fortnight at this rate (until the wife recovered and had conditions) because there was no one close to him to help them.

Time passes and the afternoon runs out. Victor enters the house, dinner is ready, the men of the house feed, take the food to Filomena, appreciate again the beauty of Raphael, light the lamp, make plans for the future and when they feel tired, decide to sleep. The next moments would be important in the lives of everyone who was part of the family.

1.12 - THREE MORE YEARS ARE OVER

Time is advancing. The Torres family is in the same financial stage as always: He lives only from family farming, which gives him when the year is good enough rainfall to survive. It was the only survival option for everyone who lived in that region, except the farmers who had more income options. In the other items, some changes: Vítor and Rafael grew up as never and unlike the fears of their parents were very close friends, they got along very well. They did everything together: they played, went to school (one was in the first and the other in the fourth grade), they arranged friends, except sometimes when there were small disagreements but that soon resolved; relatives were present a few times, usually in important events; the acquaintances and the few neighbors were only seen in social events or weekend walks, but in times of trouble the couple could only count on themselves; the elites continued to dictate the course of all, a mark of the colonelism of the time in the northeast; and the cangaceiros, known as bandits, were seen by some as heroes because they represented the struggle of a suffering and wronged people.

Even with all this happening, the family continued to walk in peace. Jilmar, as her boss, would do everything he could to ensure that her children and wife had the necessary security to progress and win, something that was not possible in her day a few years ago. Until now, he was fulfilling his role very well. However, I would only be satisfied when they were married and married, only then to rest. I wonder if I could do it. Keep up, reader.

Discovering childhood

1.13-SOME INTERESTING EXPERIENCES IN THE LIVES OF THE TWO BROTHERS

1.13.1-The mermaid case

Time moves forward a little more time. At the moment, Victor is eight years old and his brother Rafael, five. They remain friends as they once were and together, they carry out various activities. Among them, they helped in the swidden even though small; loved fishing, playing with their friends and going to bathe in the river, etc.

One day, the two were playing in front of his house, when Victor had a genius idea and decided to pass it on to his little brother.

"Rafael, my little brother, I've remembered something impressive now, and I want to show you.

"What is it? If it's like that talking fish thing, you can give up. I don't believe in tall tales anymore.

"No, this time I absolutely guarantee that it is true. Come on, you won't regret it.

That said, Victor grabs his brother Rafael by the arm, and together they run desperately in the east-central direction of the site. Filomena, who was close, advises them to be careful, but they were already far away and do not hear their warnings. On the way, they get into the woods, stray from the trail by folding to the right, and have access to an orchard. They scream, shake the dust, climb several trees, hang on the branches as if they were monkeys and savor their various fruits. You spend a lot of time enjoying these happy moments.

Anxious and tired of so much euphoria, Raphael asks when they would go to the river and Vítor replies that immediately because they could find undesirable and legendary figures of the wild forest as the Saci-Pererê, the werewolf, the mule-headless, the caboclinhas or the curupira among others and that the same with their sensory gifts would not be saved. Incredulous, Raphael asks if they exist even and as an answer hears all that is possible. Without more questions and convinced that they wanted, they descend foot before foot, from the great guava in which they were hanging and when they arrived at the ground, they return the initial direction searching for fate: The river merges.

Aided by their experiences and agility, the two boys advance rapidly on the course despite all of her natural obstacles like rocks, thorns and the hard, dry ground. Time and time again, rest. What was so interesting that Victor wanted to share with his beloved little brother friend? Maybe it was something that would add something meaningful to his life, that would distract him or even a big joke. After all, they were just children and had nothing to worry about or take seriously, unlike adults. We're close to finding out. Let's go together, readers.

Overcoming all obstacles, the Torres brothers finally arrive at the small and mysterious river of the locality after a 30-minute walk. Upon arriving, Rafael did not resin and asked:

"Where's what you wanted to show me?"

"In a little while it will appear. It is a story that our father told me and that is this: In this river, inhabits a kind of magical creature (Half woman and half fish) that uses its singing to attract men, especially fishermen. Anyone who hears your singing never returns home.

"But the mermaid exists only at sea, you fool.

"Of course, I do. However, our father said that this is one of the kinds that only exists in rivers.

"What if she uses her power to lure us in?

"There is no danger. Her singing only works for adults. Besides, the angels who protect little children are always at your side, protecting them. Look: Mine and yours are smiling now and blessing us.

Rafael looks everywhere, but as he had no extrasensory gifts nothing can see. You get a little scared, and then you calm down. Resume the conversation.

"When the bug appears, what are you going to do?

"I'm going to watch her quickly, scream and run.

"Me, too.

Time passes a little longer, Victor and Rafael waited, waited.... However, even after two hours nothing happened abnormal. They heard no movement in the water other than the piabas (Small fish), no noise was heard and no figures were visualized by the two.

Tired of waiting, Rafael asks his brother:
"Where's your famous mermaid?
"You'll see she's traveled.
"I know what happened: Our father is the greatest liar in the world, and I am the greatest fool to believe in stories of river mermaids. I'll be right there!
"Wait, I'm coming too.

This is the case of the mermaid who had been nothing more than a misinterpretation of Victor who was too attached to beliefs. Or maybe it was true and that they weren't lucky enough to meet her on the day. You're going to know. For now, they give up the idea of finding her and make their way home. They take approximately the same time to go, they reunite their mother, and she prepares a snack so that they recover their spent energies. Dad hasn't come home from the farm yet. This was an interesting day of exchanges of ideas between the two brothers.

1.13.2-The hidden treasure

On a beautiful sunny Thursday afternoon in August 1909, Vítor and his brother Rafael played as usual in the backyard of the house. At one point, they get sick of a joke and start arguing about the next fun.

"What do you suggest, Victor, about the joke? (Raphael)
"Let me see........ I'm thinking................ (Victor)
"How about that..
....

....
.... (Raphael)

"Now because it's too boring. (Victor)

You're right. It has to be something interesting and different. Besides being motivating. (Raphael)

"Oh, I know! I just remembered an old story they told me. It is the story of a pirate and his treasure known is hidden here in the place, in its vicinity. However, despite all the efforts undertaken they never managed to locate him. How about we play treasure hunt? Even if it's just a story, we get a little distracted.

"Okay, but could you tell me in detail this story before we start?

"Yes. There it goes: Legend has it that in the 17th century, an old French Corsican erred on the Pernambuco coast and was rescued by indigenous people who provided him with shelter and food. Over time, he gained their trust, learned his language, made friends, and ended up joining a beautiful Indian from the tribe. He also had access to ceremonials and one day discovered that the ornaments that were used were made of pure gold. The fact grew his ambition and from then on began to strive to discover the origin of the precious stones. After I could, I'd certainly run away and live a life free of deprivation. With his experience, he deceived the woman, knew the exact location and then began planning the robbery and escape. As the feast of worship of the forest spirits was scheduled for three days later, it decided it was the appropriate day. And so, he did. At night, as many all slept exhausted, he left his hut with his trunk, entered the closed forest and as he knew the region well, thirty minutes later he arrived at the exact spot, a cave. He entered directly, and following the data his wife had passed on, found the mine. He then gathered as much gold as possible, filled his chest, left the cave and embarked on a journey to the interior of the province, regardless of his wife, the affection, and hospitality of the other members of the tribe. Walking and resting, he crossed the municipalities of the forest zone and much of the wild until arriving exactly here, where I was born (Two hundred and eighty-five years

Discovering childhood

later). At this point, he was exhausted and so at one point stopped the shadow of a coconut tree to rest. He relaxed, leaned against his torso and started napping. From the top of the coconut tree, something snapped, but this wasn't enough to wake him up. Worse for him because within minutes, a coral snake came down from the tree, began to wander over his body and with her movement the same finally woke up. Frightened, tried to grab the snake, missed the boat and the ophidian defended itself in the form of a bite. It was his end because there was nothing to save him from the poison. Angry, he killed the animal and quickly thought of a way to hide his fortune because if he wasn't going to take advantage of it, no one would either. So, he did. Gathering his last forces and already dying, he found the proper place, dug a hole and buried his treasure. Once the mission is accomplished, it's expired. However, his soul was trapped there because as the phrase says: "You will stay where your treasure is."

"Very interesting. Liked. Let's open the treasure hunt!

"Good, good, good, good, good Let's get started right away.

"Where do we start?

"Let's look for some signs at strategic points of the site.

"If you were a pirate, where would you hide your treasure?"

"I would have two alternatives: Hide it in a virtually inaccessible and murky place or store it in a place of easy access and location, so easy that no one would have imagined it to be buried there.

"That's brilliant. What do you suggest?

"I think the first option is more likely. In the place, there are many hiding places. Maybe in one of them, it's possible that we'll find some clue that will lead us to achieve our goal.

"All right. How about we start around the place?

"Approved. Let's go!

The two, with shovels and hoes, began the search, crossing tortuous paths, all around the site. However, despite their efforts and the passage of time, they found nothing important. At one point, they were about to give up. That's when Victor had a brilliant idea:

"I already know. I've uncovered the riddle!

"You've unsure what? What the other year are you talking about?

"Reason. According to the ancients, this strip was opened centuries ago. So, this is where the Corsican passed.

"Of course. What other conclusions have you drawn?

"They also say that I was on the verge of death. So, what would be the most appropriate place for a dying miser to hide what was most important? Certainly, the first place that could house such a fortune.

"Magnificent! Genius! From what I understand, now we just move on, from the beginning of the path to the right point.

"Thank you, thank you. My intuition helped. Continue.

Overexcited, Victor and Raphael resumed the path, watching closely around the surroundings to find the exact place of the treasure and that lay the tormented soul of the Corsican. They ended up finding a small cave, and decided to start the search there.

Even fearing the dark, the poisonous animals, and the souls, the two entered it, advanced in the galleries, and at one point, they took something, which made them stop. Even with the low light, they discovered a skull and with the fright, immediately left the cave that was located in the north-central of the site. Already outside, they began to dialogue:

"We need to go back and keep looking for the trunk. I think we're close. (Victor)

"You're right. That skull must belong to the cordon. (Raphael)

"Brilliant deduction, Rafael. If it is true, then the chest must be buried just below its carcass because it was weak and weakened.

"Maybe......... Let's gather our courage, go back to the gallery and dig a hole in the place as soon as possible.

"Challenge accepted. Let's go!

Making the decision, quickly, the two enter the gallery of the cave, and a while later reach the same point where they were. With the instruments, they carried and aided by their little arms, they began to remove the land from the site. After a certain period, they hit a hard surface which provoked cries from both:

"Wow! It's the gold!

They removed more land, and shortly thereafter removed a chest from the resounding hole of satisfaction. They carried it out and when they opened it, they visualized countless gold stones. However, Victor, with his ingenuity and little experience, was sad and closed the chest. He explained to his little brother:

"This is not real gold. It's fool's gold," he said.

"Are you certain? We've had so much work. (Raphael)

"I do. I believe that the real gold shines much more than this because I had the opportunity to see a piece on the neck of a town owner.

"What a pity! I had so much hope of changing my life.

"Don't worry about it. We're worth our works and ethics, not vile metal. Even without him, we'll be happy.

"You're right.

Low and disappointed, they buried the chest again in the same place. They left the cave, made their way back and finally went home. They would continue their normal life, in the means to difficulties and trials, but together with their parents they would remain a special united family. The Torres family.

1.13.3-A different joke

It was the year 1909, the month of September and the Torres family continued with their saga in the wild Pernambuco, specifically in the Fundão site, rural area of the municipality of Cimbres (Present-day Pesqueira). Jilmar, chief, took care of the work in the swidden at harvest time and in the off-season, he was spouting other land. Agriculture was the only thing he knew how to do because he had no opportunity to have any education. The same case of his wife Filomena who because she was a woman worked as a housewife and lace maker. Both were destitute when they married and remained humble and happy. The couple's children, Vítor, nine, and Rafael, six, continued to be an example of companionship and friendship, although disagreements sometimes occurred between the two. But this was absolutely normal in any relationship.

One day, in front of the house, the two played hide-and-seek, masked boy. However, after the three games, they got a little tired. They decided to stop. They laid on the grass (next to each other) and dozed off. Upon awakening, Rafael again got agitated and pulled conversation with his brother Victor.

"How about we make up a different joke?

"That's nice. Do you have any suggestions?

"I do. How about we hang from a tree upside down to see who could last the longest?

"It's a good idea. But I think it's too dangerous. We'll do it when you get a little bigger. I thought of something: Wouldn't it be better to play wheel, inventing characters along the way?

"I don't agree. I'm small, and I don't have much imagination. I'd be a fool and, in the end, you'd be like,

"That's all right. Let me think better then..
....
.... I know, I know. We'll play cop and bandit, something we've never done.

"What's this joke like?

"You're the bad guy, and I'm the cop. You run, I wait ten seconds and I chase you. If I catch up with you, I'll slap you. Then, in the second phase, we'll turn the papers around, and you can get back at me.

"Sounds nice. We never really did. Can we get started?

"Yes.

Rafael runs desperate. Victor mentally counts the seconds and when it reaches number ten it also shoots. For his older age and agility, he reaches his brother quickly, grabs him, calls him a ban-

Discovering childhood

dit, knocks him to the ground and gives him some slaps. Unintentionally, some hit Rafael with violence and make him cry. Unreformed, Raphael stands up, turns his back and shouts to the whole universe to hear:

" I'm not a bandit. I'm just a kid!

Brother's attitude moved Victor. Pushy tears run down his face, approach him, hug him, apologize for the brutality and say he is critical in his life after all. The strategy works. He recovers and both decide to stop to avoid further embarrassment. They return home, feed, do other leisure activities and at the end of the day sleep peacefully already thinking about the adventures of the next day. Fate was building day after day.

1.13.4-The accident

It was St. John's Night of the year 1910. As tradition dictates, the Torres family prepared the bonfire and all the typical foods of this time of year. They then gathered the whole family, offered lunch and dinner, put the conversations up to date and finally went to light the fire in front of the house.

During a good period, they paid tribute to the saint, ate snacks, made promises, talked a little more and when the campfire finished burning, most of those present went to sleep. It was just Victor and Raphael, playing around the campfire. At one point, Victor stop, and pulls conversation with his little brother.

"Have you ordered?

"No. What about you?

"Not either. How about we do it now?

"That's all right. I'm going to ask the saint never to lack food for the people of the interior of the Northeast.

"What a difficult request. But show your big heart. For my part, I will ask for greater control over my gift, courage to face adversity, be happy in my future, and prosperity and health for my entire family. We must ratify our request with great action.

"What kind?

"To demonstrate our faith and trust in the saint, we must challenge physical laws, such as passing over the embers of the fire. However, this requires a little concentration. Will you come with me?

"If there's no danger, let's go.

Quickly, Victor strolled over the campfire a little asleep, in leaps, and succeeded. Rafael, by inexperience, was a little more time-consuming, and when he left, he was in tears. The suit caught everyone's attention. Filomena scolded Victor, and both went to try to ease her younger brother's pain. They used some water and luckily the burns weren't so severe. When he got better, he went to bed and sleep. The lesson is also contained in the Bible: "Thu shall not temp the Lord his God."

1.14-THE DISCOVERY OF LOVE

1.14.1-First experiences

Vítor's routine, at the time, at the age of ten, included working in the garden helping his father in the morning, in the afternoon playing games with his brother Rafael and sometimes visits neighbors and relatives, primarily on weekends. In one of these visits, she approached Sara more (Girl of her same age who had as characteristics brown eyes, defined and delicate feature, thin and well done body, black hair made in locks and was the daughter of Professor Genoveva) and between both began to emerge a strong feeling that can be called childish love translated into hand given, kisses on the face, hugs and the mutual will to always be together. But everything was done in secret because they were afraid of their parents' reaction and together, they discovered this wonderful feeling.

Discovering childhood

After discovering their affinity for each other, they got closer and started hanging out together. So, they discovered a little of the world and this feeling so beautiful, although the precaution came first because of the prejudices of the time. If they were discovered, and the separation occurred, they would not regret the experience gained. Their luck was cast.

1.14.2-The meeting in the Church

The beginning of the relationship between Sara and Victor was windy in pomp despite some disagreements. However, these moments were logos overcome. After a few departures, Victor sent a note to be delivered in his wife's hands, through one of his friends named Caio. The same quickly went to Sara's house, and upon arriving at the destination said he would talk to her. Without distrust, Genoveva called the daughter who when she attended Caio, received the note, thanked and said goodbye. Hiding the paper, she locked herself in the room and went to read it. Here's the content:

Beloved Sara

I wanted to invite you on a date with me to be together and talk a little more. How about if you show up at church today at 4:00 p.m.? Even without knowing your answer, and I look forward to this place and time. Sincerely, Victor.

After reading it, Sara thought a little and concluded that it would not hurt any to leave the house a little and find again with the sweet boy who was The Victor. He planned the best excuse to be given to his mother, and at the agreed time, he left for the small chapel of the site, founded by the Franciscans two years ago.

At the exact time, she entered the room, and when the two saw each other, they immediately ran for a long, gentle embrace. On this occasion, the friar had arrived, caught them both, but did not rebuke them. On the contrary, he thought it was beautiful and promised to keep it a secret. From the Church, the two set out to play as two children they were and get to know each other better. Every once in a while, a kiss would come out. In this climate, they spent the rest of the afternoon and during saying goodbye, they arranged a new meeting for the next week. Would this bonanza remain? Keep up, reader.

1.14.3-The brief period of separation

After the church meeting, Victor and Sara would remain separated for approximately one week to take care of their personal lives and not to arouse the attention of the adults involved. During this period, Vítor took care of the swidden, helped with some housework, played with his brother Rafael, went out with friends, strolled at the house of relatives. Sara helped her mother home, played with her friends, went to town and read a book. But neither left even a moment the memory of the moments together, although it was nothing serious. It was just a pure, chilly feeling that had no major worries.

The two were willing to continue living this beautiful experience, through which many people go through, the first flirting, the first uncompromising look, the coexistence and all this occurring even in childhood. Where would this in the end take them? They neither suspected nor were they worried about the future. The important thing was to live every moment of the present intensely as unique or as if it were the last.

1.14.4-An important date

One week after the last meeting, Vítor and Sara would finally meet at an important social event for everyone who lived on the Fundão site. It was the date of ten years of the founding of his school, the rural municipal school Pleasure to learn. Present since the foundation, Professor Genoveva Garcia organized everything aided by her only daughter Sara.

Discovering childhood

On the agreed date and time, Vítor, accompanied by his family, arrived at the home of his former teacher and his beloved Sara. As they were long-known, Victor and his family entered unceremoniously, greeted all present and sat at one of the tables set. They waited a while until the band of fife arrived and began to cheer the party. Then couples began to emerge for dance, more guests arrive, the movement is intense and when everyone is distracted, Victor and Sara move and meet outside. When they meet, they hug, kiss on the face, hold hands and go play. They invent a thousand and one games, Rafael arrives, joins the group and together live exciting moments.

After they get tired of playing, they talk a little about their life, and one goes on passing on experiences to each other despite their young age. Exhausted the conversation, they return to the house, to enjoy a little the festivities. They integrate their respective families, eat a little, and have fun in the best possible way. In the end, they say goodbye and promise to see each other again soon. Vítor returns home with his family and Sara goes to sleep. Keep up, reader.

1.14.5-The Day of the Indian

Time passes a little and arrives specifically on April 19, 1911, Indian Day. This date is very celebrated in the rural area of Cimbres (Current Pesqueira), including the Fundão site that is close to one of the Xucuru villages of the region, the first local inhabitants. By unanimous decision of the heads of the village, an open invitation was sent to all nearby residents to attend the tribe to celebrate together with the indigenous people on this symbolic date. Many families at the Fundão site accepted the proposal, including the Garcia and Torres families. This was another opportunity for coexistence between Victor and Sara.

Two hours before the agreed time, the Torres, and Garcia families left for the village, met on the way, and remained walking together for the rest of the journey. On the way, they exchanged experiences and expectations about the unique and unusual meeting that awaited them. What good would you take from those special moments? They would certainly have a lot to learn from a millennial people who are the true owners of Brazil. Besides, they had a lot to teach, too. It would be the perfect exchange between the races although on a day-to-day and day-to-day life they already had a lot of contact. Soon, they continued the journey without major worries.

Exactly at the scheduled time, they arrived in the village, entered, were greeted by the hosts and when everything was ready, the party began. Had it all: Typical dances, religious rituals, music, abundant food, speeches, games.

Vítor, Rafael and Sara moved away from the adults taking advantage to make friends with the Little Indian. Victor, a little dazzled, demonstrated his hidden powers that grew every day. Everyone applauded him. Then they played like normal kids. At one point, Victor and Sara were left alone. They talked, made plans, held hands without arousing any further suspicion. An instant later, they reintegrated into the group and continued to have fun.

By evening, the party ended, the visitors thanked and said goodbye, and finally left. They took about the same time on the way back, sometimes stopping for the rest of the animals. Arriving home, Genoveva and Sara said goodbye to Victor, and family, and they walked a little further. Later, they come home too. They immediately went to sleep and Victor did not stop thinking about his new friends and the pleasant company of Sara. Would they still have contact? The same cares a little about it, but soon is overcome by the tiredness of the trip. Fate was cast.

1.14.6- The day of independence

1.14.6.1-historical context

On September 7, 1822, on the banks of the Ipiranga, a black chapter was concluded in our history: Portuguese political domination. Since their arrival in our country, foreigners have focused their main resources on colonization and not colonization itself. They did everything: They enslaved the indigenous peoples (The real Brazilians), destroyed part of our fauna and flora, extracted our ores among other losses. This only ended on this day.

But independence was not built only in front of the Ipiranga River. It was a slow and complicated process of which were of valuable participation to patriots. Among them, it is worth mentioning: Tomás Antônio Gonzaga, Claudio Manuel da Costa, Domingos Vidal da Costa, Joaquim José da Silva Xavier and Joaquim Silvério dos Reis (Minas Conspiracy); João de Deus do Nascimento, Manuel Faustino dos Santos, Luiz Gonzaga das Virgens and Lucas Dantas (Revolt of tailors); Antônio Carlos, José Bonifácio de Andrada e Silva, José da Silva Lisboa, Joaquim Gonçalves Ledo and Januário da Cunha Barbosa (Political articulators, the latter two of which worked in masonic newspapers and shops), culminating in the act of September 7, 1822.

And you reader, one might ask: After this day, everything was settled? The answer is no. We were only partly independent. Overall, everything was absolutely the same: We continued to depend on foreign aid from other countries, maintained an economic structure based on slave labor, and the elites took the time to take power at the expense of the popular classes. Result: Revolts that were stifled thanks to the dictatorial power of the emperor.

Even with the passage of the decades and with the advent of the republic, we still carried latent difficulties in our economic-social development because it was not only the political regime the problem but a range of very complex factors included corruption, little emphasis on health and education, drought, discrimination in its various aspects.

We can say that Ipiranga's cry was only the initial milestone of a long process of evolution of our society and we are currently an example to the world for our economy, our natural resources, by our strength and our nature, despite the great social inequalities that exist. We are the country of the present and the future and it is up to us to continue to be proud of our land.

1.14.6.2-Continuation of history

It was September 7, 1911. Traditionally, the date was celebrated at the headquarters of the municipality Pesqueira with a large parade. All known or unknown characters of the founding site have prepared for the party. Among them, the families-focus of the moment: Torres and Garcia. After preparing the body, they met on the road and left together (With the members mounted on horseback). On the way, they met other families, forming a large procession taking advantage of the trip to exchange ideas and bring the latest news up to speed. They remained at this rate for two hours until arriving in the city's central square.

Upon arriving at the destination, they joined a large crowd waiting for the parade and the band. When it passed, everyone followed. Vítor and Sara enjoyed a moment of distraction from the adults and went out to play and talk. Approximately twenty minutes of coexistence passed, exchanged caresses and at the end of this time decided to return to the procession. They continued with their parents until the end.

After the festivities, had a quick snack, rode back on the horses and started their way back. They took approximately the same time on the way, went to their homes and rested the rest of the day. They had fulfilled their role as citizens once again.

1.14.7-The tour

Time moves a little further. The end of the year arrives (1911) bringing with him the school recess. At this time, Genoveva has a brilliant idea in order to provide fun and keep busy the students, alumni and the general staff of the site Fundão: Take a tour to a special place located in the neighboring site, a cave that had served as a dwelling for prehistoric man evidenced through the traces of his passage (Cave Paintings).

And so, he did. He sent the invitations and as he received the endorsement, he was hiring the carriages. When you reached enough people, you marked the date and time. When the day and time arrived, all attended in front of the contractor's house (Genoveva). The means of locomotion were appearing, crowding and leaving. The latter, coincidentally, was filled in by members of the Torres and Garcia family. As they were known, the entire trip would certainly be filled with tasty and enriching conversations. Time went ahead, the carriages and people faced the scorching sun, the gigantic dust, the challenges of a loss-making road, but no one who was making the trip complained because fate was attractive enough to make up for it.

Two hours after departure, one by one the carriages were arriving at the destination, parking, and the passengers descending with their respective backpacks. When they all arrived, they gathered in groups of five and entered the cave. When it came the turn of the group composed of the families Garcia and Torres (The last), they had the opportunity to see more calmly all the beauties of the place composed of stalactites and stalagmites, the thought-provoking dark, the stones, the sculptures and rock formations, in addition to the paintings of prehistoric men representing various situations between them, hunting, sex, religion, society , i.e. culture in general. They spent about half an hour inside the little cave.

On leaving, they had a picnic with some northeastern delights and all participated. The moment the adults got a little distracted, Sara and Victor got away and went to play, exchange caresses and talk. The problem was, it took them a long time this time. They were searched and discovered by their families. Genoveva did not like anything, pushed them both away, did not let go of her daughter and ended the tour. They then returned to the carriages and started their way back. It took approximately the same time to go, facing the same obstacles. Arriving at the site, everyone said goodbye and returned to their respective homes, rested a little, took care of their obligations and when night, went to sleep. What would be, from now on, of Sara and Victor's relationship? Keep up, reader.

1.14.8 - The mismatch

The day after the tour, Vítor was anxious and distressed at the possibility of estrangement from his beloved Sara. After all the experiences lived alongside her, she had become a more docile and behaved boy, something she did not want to miss. Thinking about the problem caused by the discovery of the two, he ended up having an idea to find his beloved: Send another note by his friend Gaius, addressed to her. Making the decision, sat on the edge of his little table, picked up pen and ink and wrote a few brief lines. When he finished, he searched for the young man already mentioned and upon finding him, handed him the ticket and gave precise instructions.

Immediately, Gaius went to Sara's house, and with his firm and safe steps it did not take long to arrive. He then approached a little further, slammed the door of the house, waited a few moments, the door opened, and was attended to by Genoveva. Asked about the reason for the visit, Gaius told her that he wanted to speak to Sara. No same moment, Genoveva became suspicious and said that she was not but that she could settle for her. Out of naivety, Gaius handed him the note and left. Genoveva then took the opportunity. He read all the content and did not like mainly because he came from Vítor.

Discovering childhood

Genoveva reflected for a few moments the situation and took a drastic action: She took the note, and imitated the letters of Victor, replaced it with another. He took him to Sara's room and delivered it. When reading it, the little girl had a shock because she did not recognize the boy who until recently had fun. But he had no doubt: He was himself. The content was as follows:

Dear Sara,

I thought it over. We are very young and it would be good to give a stop in our meetings. I do it honestly because I don't have any more fun with your presence even though you're special. Maybe we're just still friends.

A hug and I hope you'll forget me at once, remember your mother. Carefully, Victor.

Sara's reaction was not good: She screamed, scoffed, cried, and punched the wall. Attracted by the scream, her mother entered the room, comforted her and took advantage of her daughter's difficult moment to suggest that they move to a municipality far away, where she had already been offered a good job. Without thinking straight, Sara accepted the proposal and Genoveva said she would get the details right. Two weeks later, the two left without saying goodbye, in search of their new destiny. What would happen? Let's continue the narrative.

1.15- THE NEW ROUTINE

After Sara's departure, Victor spent a season in depression, wondering what he had done wrong. However, he gradually became convinced that it was not at fault. He and his beloved had been victims of a cruel conspiracy of fate. Although the relationship was extinguished, it had been worth the experiences lived and who knows when they were adults, they could rediscover themselves, find out how they feel for each other really and start over. Although this was a remote possibility at the time because the two of them were gone in the world.

Over time, Vítor was choking the memories and getting quieter. When he was fully recovered, he returned to his normal routine: Work on his father's site performing various rural activities (In the morning), housework helping his mother (afternoon), rest at night, games and leisure activities on the weekend along with his brother Rafael, friends and neighbors. It would be happy in your simple and routine life, but thought-provoking and interesting.

The other members of his family continued in the same way as always: Jilmar, with his continued dedication to rural work, his mother taking care of the house, his crafts, the family in general and his brother Rafael had finished the primary school and next year would begin to help in the treatment of the swidden, in addition to having time for his games , of course. Everything was going well until now despite the growing difficulties that a poor country family had to face.

1.16-THE STORIES OF FILOMENA

At the age of eleven and eight, one of them being almost a pre-teenager, Vítor and Rafael had assimilated many values passed on by their parents, specifically through the figure of their mother, Filomena, who was more present. One of the ways to pass on this knowledge was through small illustrative but wise stories. I'll transcribe some I've heard of.

1.16.1-The animal boy

Diego was the boy of an upper-class family in the city of Recife. Despite the good financial condition and good basis of values received, the same was restless, smart and disobedient to parents who struggled at all times to make him a good boy. While he did not remediate or regret his antics.

One fine day, he made a bad trick and his mother, angry, made one last attempt to correct him: He slapped him. Immediately, the boy reacted, grabbed his mother's legs and bit them. At this moment, the same, inspired by the great pain and hurt caused by the son, said: Acting in this way, you do not even look like a child but an animal. The plague caught on time.

From this day, every full moon night, as punishment, Diego transformed: Leave the house irrationally howling like a wolf. The curse would last as long as he lived for him to learn to respect a mother.

1.16.2-The papa liver

Long ago, there was a very distant kingdom, a prince named Mimoso. His main feature was the unmeasured ambition and his parents, who loved him very much, struggled to meet all his requirements: They had already bought him more than 100,000 imported toys and more than a thousand pieces of gold. However, nothing they did satisfied him. One day, the prince came to the height of asking for ten silver stars from heaven and drove his parents mad: What would they do to meet such an absurd request?

They reflected, reflected....... and they decided that instead of ten silver stars in the sky, I would give him the same number of stars. However, handmade. When they went to deliver the gift, the boy took the stars, threw them to the ground, braved and snort in anger, said it was not his request. The king then replied:

"My son, me, and your mother, try our best to please you. However, what you asked for is humanly impossible to achieve. Any child would want to be in his place and win this kind of gift.

The boy did not conform and outraged and indignant fled towards the neighboring forest. As he entered the middle of the vegetation and advanced a little, he sat under a tree, lowered his head and cried convulsively. Wrapped in his pain, he didn't even notice a stranger's approach.

The creature was the legendary old papa-liver that fed on the organ of the same name as the little children. Suddenly, the animal caught the prince shouting:

"Now I'm going to eat your liver!

Frightened and lost, the prince began to scream for help but no one answered him. That's when an inner voice told him:

"You should be at home with your parents who love you so much and instead of crying you should smile and thank for the life God has given you.

Right now, he regretted being so selfish. In the midst of the squeeze, he wished to return home. As if it were by magic, the papa-liver disappeared and Mimoso ran back to the palace. When he arrived, he hugged his parents, thanked him for the gift, but he didn't accept it. He decided to donate everything to the poor children of the kingdom and never again dared to ask his parents for anything extravagant. On the contrary, he was content with what he received willingly from them.

1.16.3-The best prize

Upon a time, there was a boy named Ronaldo who lived nearby of Salvador. Like most of the population of the region, his family was destitute and survived the dump in which he worked eight hours a day to help his parents and himself in their basic needs. In the few moments of leisure, he improvised toys with garbage residues such as balls, shuttlecocks, and carts. Even with all these difficulties, I still dreamed of better days.

The special characteristics that this boy gathered made him an example for everyone who knew him. Some examples of his beautiful attitudes were: He had participated in the campaign of the sweater and Christmas without hunger (He was the poster boy and did not charge any cache for it), besides encouraging the merchants of the time to give a part of their profit to the poor.

His life story gained such connotation that it reached the ears of a certain Santa Claus. Analyzing his case, he decided to help him and exactly on December 25, Christmas date, this good old man arrived at the shack where Ronaldo lived. Upon arriving, he observed in the surrounding area and verified that there was no chimney because the address was basic. As a last alternative, he decided to put the gift he brought against the door. Once that's done, he's gone.

The other day, in the morning, the child woke up. From the bedroom he went to the living room. As he tried to get through the door, he bumped into the package. Full of curiosity, he tore up the envelope and found a letter and a form. However, as she could not read, she called her mother and asked her to translate the content into it. She read, did not believe, reread to make sure and told her son that there was written that the same from the year that was to begin would be entitled to a full scholarship in the best school in the city. In addition, the family would receive a monthly basic basket and medical follow-up. All this good news was described in the letter.

Already on the form, he received a congratulatory message, praising him for his achievements (Signed by Santa Claus in question). After reading, Ronaldo and his mother hugged and thanked God for still having angels on earth. It was the best Christmas present Ronaldo and his family could get.

1.16.4-The value of work

There was a worker bee called Zunzum. Its job was basically to visit thousands of flowers daily searching for nectar, the main ingredient with which honey is produced. To reach a significant amount of honey it takes a lot of work from worker bees: An intense shuttle from the hive to the raw material (Sometimes they travel several kilometers away at a time).

One day, a man named Abilio, who specializes in removing honey, approached the hive. He wore a special costume to protect him from the stings and also brought with him material to smoke the environment and confuse enemies. At the right time, he attacked the bees with his smoke to make them dizzy and disoriented. Zunzum then exclaimed:

"Why are you doing this? Do you want to kill us on purpose?"

"I don't want to kill them; my goal is just to remove the honey.

"It is not fair: It was my sisters and me who strive to produce and package the content in the alveolus.

"I don't care. I want your honey; I will sell one part and consume another because it is very nutritious and appreciated.

"If you dare to take him, we'll sting you.

"You can't sting me. I'm protected.

"Monster, don't you have feelings or remorse? If you catch our honey, my sisters and I will die of star fire.

"That's your problem. I had nothing to do with it.

"This is an outrage, a swindle to the law.

"The law I know is this: It is called the law of the strongest, of survival.

In saying this, you didn't listen to the bee anymore. He removed all the honey from the hive and left back for his home. Once again, the man animal showed its superiority and primacy over all living beings.

1.16.5-Beauty and tuning do not set on the table

The owner of a circus was looking for a special animal that knew tricks and with that stood out. Searching for this goal, he went into the forest, walked a certain distance, pasted posters announcing what he was looking for, and waited a while. The first one that appeared was the peacock:

I hear you're looking for a star because you know you've already found it. There is no other animal that equals me: My beauty is exalted by painters and poets, I have elegance, style, and a lot of charm.

The man watched the animal from top to bottom and replied:

"I'm sorry, but this isn't what I'm looking for.

The second to appear was the turkey:

"You don't have to look for anyone else. From today, I will be your main attraction because I'm a great singer.

Again, the man observed the candidate, thought a little and replied:

"Excuse me, I'm not looking for singers. I already have a mermaid who has a great voice in my circus.

The third (a) candidate (a) who appeared was a chicken:

"Are you looking for a star? Yes, you did. I am very talented: Dance tango, funk, axé, forró, samba, ballroom dance.

"All right. I'll take a test with you. If it is not approved, it will give at least one soup.

That said, he grabbed her, came out of the woods and headed to the circus. With this unusual outcome, the peacock and turkey exclaimed relieved:

"I'm so sure he didn't pick us.

1.17 - THE CODE OF CONDUCT OF FILOMENA

Aided by her life experience and wisdom, Filomena developed a code of conduct for her children verbally so that she could guide them on the paths of life. This code was little understood by the two and on their initiative, they drafted the rules. Here's the code:

1. When lifting
    1.1-Prepare and organize the room (Make the bed, sweep the room, dust the furniture);
    1.2-Bathing;
    1.3-Assist in the preparation and breakfast;
    1.4-Brush your teeth and comb your hair (Do not suck a bullet or take dust);

1.5-Go to school (Partly completed task, had already completed primary school);
2. Upon arrival from school or work
    2.1-Store school supplies in an appropriate place;
    2.2-Remove the school uniform (Do not need or bend);
    2.3-Bath again, change clothes and have lunch, chewing slowly to better digest food;
    2.4-In meals, know how to behave at a table;
    2.5-Leisure time: studying, playing with colleagues, sightseeing, etc.;
    2.6-Help in housework.
3. At night
    3.1-Talk to parents when you have any problems (Questions, problems, etc...)
    3.2-Dinner (Following the same rules as lunch);
    3.3-Bathing;
    3.4-Pray to God and the guardian angel, thanking for another day of life;
    3.5-Go to bed early.
4. Socially
    4.1-Respect and help older people;
    4.2-Keep quiet while adults talk;
    4.3-Show education and sympathy at all times;
    4.4-Always seek to demonstrate your love and understanding;
5. General

5.1-Fulfill the obligations at about the same time.

1.18-HUNTER STORIES

It was May 4, 1912, a Saturday. On that day, it was common for the Torres family to receive a visit from an old acquaintance named Francisco, or rather Chico, a hunter famous in the region for his talent in telling stories. That's how it happened.

Discovering childhood

Old Chico slammed the door. Jilmar went to meet him inviting him in. Together, they went to the small room of the house where Filomena, Vítor and Rafael were already located. He greeted everyone and sat on an available stool. Jilmar started the dialogue.

"Hey, Chico, all right? We've known each other for a long time. Since we moved to this place, but despite our contact, you're still a figure full of mysteries. To hear you're from the back, don't you?

"Yes, I was born in Cabrobó, I loved my land, and I never wanted to get away from it. But I suffered a lot from my stepfather's beatings, and one day I reacted, stabbed him, he fell unconscious, and I ran away. I don't know what happened to him or my mother. Then I went around the world. I arrived by chance at this place and decided to settle here- he replied.

"I Understand. You learned how to craft lies? (Jilmar)
"With no one. I learned from my experiences. (The same)
"Do you have anything to tell us today? (Victor)
"Yes, several. Do you like my stories? (Chico)
"Yes, a lot. (Victor)
"Me, too. (Raphael)
"Don't impress the boys, Chico. (Filomena)
"It's okay. I'll be careful. Let's go? (Francisco)

Everyone accepted the invitation. They took his lanterns and followed him. They went through the whole hut reaching the outside area. On their way out, they gazed at the stars, but soon lost attention to it only to focus on the hunter's mysterious figure. Then he started.........................

1.18.1-The spirit of the forest

When I was young and I lived there to the sides of Cabrobó, I used to go out on Saturdays. I usually went to the countryside to hunt. I love doing that. It was and it's my leisure. One day, caught in the forest, I was lurking the game ready to give the boat (Silent and attentive looking for the best way to catch my prey). At this moment, full of anxiety and nervousness came to me the urge to look back. In making this movement, behold, the figure of a mulatto girl appears in front of me, with long, drained hair and Brown eyes. He looked at me from top to bottom and in a serious and rude voice said:

"Don't shoot. I won't let you kill any animals.

"Why is that? God gave us the animals so that they can help us and serve as food.

"That's right, that's right. But God reserved this day. He's sacred. So, you can give up and leave.

"I get it. I understand your point of view and I promise I won't break this law. You can leave it. I'm out of here.

That said, the mulatto is gone. I left immediately. Next time, I'd hunt on a weekday so I wouldn't risk missing the trip.

1.18.2-The salvation of the child

One day, I was coming out of the woods, coming from a profitable hunt (He brought with me, in my bag, three preás and some birds) and with this success, I was happy in life. As I was saying, I was walking quietly through the woods, in its final part, when suddenly (not far from there) I heard cries of despair and pain (It sounded like a child's voice). Made by mercy, without thinking, he immediately addressed me to meet the afflicted voice with the aim of soothing it. Further on, I folded to the right, found a row of trees, and advancing a little I came across the following scene: A Boa Constrictor snake (approximately three meters long) wrapped its tail in the trunk of a plant, and at the other end, its thirsty mouth clung to a fragile, thin leg that struggled in vain to loosen.

The owner of the leg was a black child (about eight years old), probably the son of African descendants from an extinct quilombo near there. As I saw her agony, I approached and tried to help her in the best way Possible: I removed the machete from my waist and set myself to injure the venomous snake. She backed off a little bit. Then I grabbed the ends of her mouth and pressed her to let the child go. I fought bravely for twenty minutes until she gave in: Overcome and exhausted by tiredness, she gave up her prey. I threw some rocks at it and finally she went into the closed woods and walked away permanently.

The boy (Free and relieved), sighed gratefully:
"You saved my life.
"God helped me. Now calm down and wash that wound so it doesn't get infected.
"How can I express my gratitude?
"Just do this: Never enter the woods alone. You could have died.
"It's all right. You must be my guardian angel.
"Angel, I'm not. Certainly, your protector has guided me here: What has just happened is a real miracle.

We said goodbye and never saw him again. That's the lesson.

1.18.3-The ounce

In the interior of Paraiba, there are a lot of ounces. When you're in the forest of the region, doing any activity, you run the risk of meeting any of them. That's what happened one day. It happened as follows: I was hunting deer along with my faithful dog, on the stakeout. What was not our surprise (Instead of the deer appeared an ounce). By the way she acted, she seemed to be starving (She walked slowly and silently sniffing out the possible prey in all directions). Seeing her, my heart almost stopped. Moments later, I recovered my calm and reflected in order to decide quickly what to do. But there was no time. Impulsively, my dog barked and set off towards the feline. In response, she applied a slight paw to him to keep him away. With that, I took out the rifle and was about to shoot the bug. Sensing the danger, she said:

"Don't shoot. I have puppies to raise.

"Why shouldn't I shoot? You hurt my best friend. Besides, she's a competitor in the hunt.

"Your friend attacked me first. I just made myself defend myself. As for hunting, I need her to feed me and my cubs.

"I get it. Then I'll let you go. But beware of other hunters.

"Thank you, thank you.

I decided to stop the hunt and returned with my dog to my house. The jaguar was really angry, but if it wasn't provoked, it didn't pose much danger. At least this one I met.

1.19 - FAREWELL

After telling these stories, Chico changed the subject and talked for a time about politics, economics, popular news and gossip with members of the Torres family. Exhausted the affairs, he said goodbye and went to his house with the aim of sleeping. Next Saturday, I'd probably come back and infect everyone with your sympathy. I would therefore continue to make history.

After his departure, the members of the Torres family also went to sleep because they came from a long and tiring day. In the coming days, they would remain in their simple but thought-provoking and dignified life. They were an example of struggle and perseverance in the region against all the phenomena of his time, especially Victor who every day saw his powers grow and develop without anyone who would advise him. What would be of the same and your valued family? Keep up, reader.

1.20 - END OF CHILDHOOD

It was August 1, 1912. Vítor had turned twelve years old, the final milestone of his childhood. In this brief period, he had lived many intense experiences. The most important were the birth of the brother, the discovery of spiritual gifts, the routine, the values learned from the parents, the childish love provoked by Sara. All that had lived added wisdom, humility, and patience to its virtues, which was already a

Discovering childhood

good beginning of evolution. Now, he would live a new phase, adolescence, the second of his life.

Still in the first, he had lived the fear of the dark, of the ghosts; had overcome its sensory limits, trying to understand the hidden forces; had innovated and created new games with his brother Rafael; he had discovered the attraction and the like as a child, which was not common; Let us now move on to adolescence and adulthood.

End

www.ingramcontent.com/pod-product-compliance
Lightning Source LLC
LaVergne TN
LVHW040202080526
838202LV00042B/3282